For Summer and Millie

"I am going to find a Dragon" said the princess one day.
"I shan't be too long; I will be on my way".
"A Dragon?!" said the King with a smile on his face.
"You won't find one here. Not in this place."

"Well, there must be one and it cannot be far."
And she went out the door with a wave and "Ta ta".

She strolled out the castle and into the town,
With all the people staring at her crown.
The Mayor asked "Princess, why are you here all alone?"
"Do I need to get your parents on the phone?"
The Mayor was quite old and was rather tall
"There is no need to give my parents a call".
"A Dragon is the thing that I must find".
And she wandered off, leaving him behind.

She strolled out of the town and onto a path,
Where she found a Witch, who was taking a bath.
"Hello Princess, why are you in this place so remote?"
She said this whilst cleaning her back with green soap.
"I am finding a Dragon" she replied, covering her eyes.
"So I will bid you a fair well, good day and goodbye".
"Well, good luck!" said the Witch as she cleaned out her ears.
"There hasn't been a Dragon round these parts for years!"
The Princess just shrugged and went on some more,
Wondering what else she might see on her tour.

She carried on further and came to a hole,
And there at the bottom was a big smelly Troll.
"Princess." he said in a very croaky voice,
"Why are you here, is it by choice?"
"Yes" she replied skipping past the Troll's pit,
"I'm off to find a Dragon, I'll see you in a bit".

"A Dragon?" he snickered as she went on her way.
"I bet you won't find one by the end of today!"

She skipped on and on, and on a bit more,
Until she heard a deafening roar.
"A Dragon!" she thought, as she crept on ahead.
A part of her wanted to turn back instead.
The noise seemed to come from a cave she could see.
"A Dragon's in there, it really must be!"
The roaring was so loud that both her knees shook,
But she was very brave and snuck a quick look.

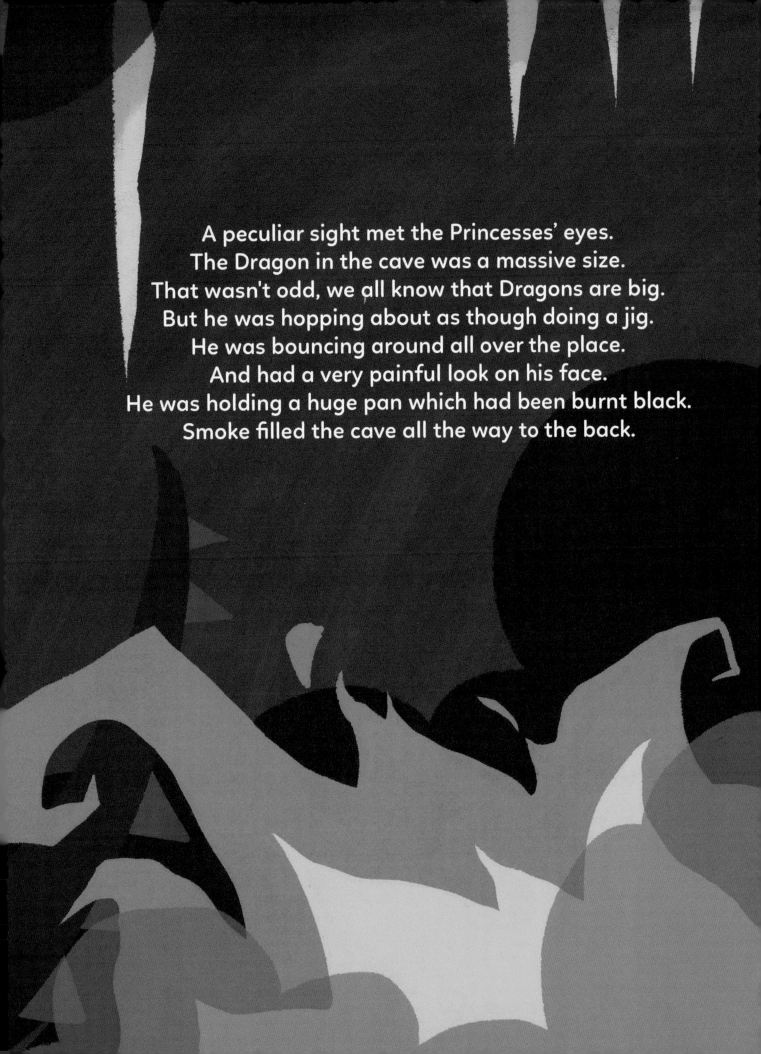

A peculiar sight met the Princesses' eyes.
The Dragon in the cave was a massive size.
That wasn't odd, we all know that Dragons are big.
But he was hopping about as though doing a jig.
He was bouncing around all over the place.
And had a very painful look on his face.
He was holding a huge pan which had been burnt black.
Smoke filled the cave all the way to the back.

"My toe" he roared. "My toe, oh boohoo."
"I have ruined my dinner, now what do I do?"
The Princess felt bad, "Don't worry I can help."
She surprised the Dragon who gave out a yelp.
"I can help" she repeated "But please, oh please, don't eat me"
The Dragon sighed "I was going to have vegetables for my tea."
"Not all dragons eat people, they taste a bit weird."
"Especially when you get one with a big bushy beard."
"They are crunchy, chewy and not at all yum."
"It is fruit and veg that I want in my tum."

The Princess did not expect to meet a Dragon quite like this.
One who ate carrots, was there something she'd missed?
But as she bandaged his toe, he said that he liked to draw.
And he would rather sing than let out a roar.
They joked and they laughed and got on very well.
This Dragon is awesome, the Princess could tell.

It was starting to get dark out, the light was getting dimmer.
The Princess said "I must get home or my I will miss my dinner.
I didn't realise it was so late, I will have to hurry.
My parents are probably starting to worry."
The Dragon said "Relax, you will be home in a snap."
"I'll fly you there now, climb on my back"

The Princess climbed on; she was excited to fly.
The Dragon leapt from the cave and took to the sky.
Up they soared and did a loop the loop.
The Princess laughed and let out a "Whoop".
The Princess looked down; everything was so small.
She held on tight, being careful not to fall.

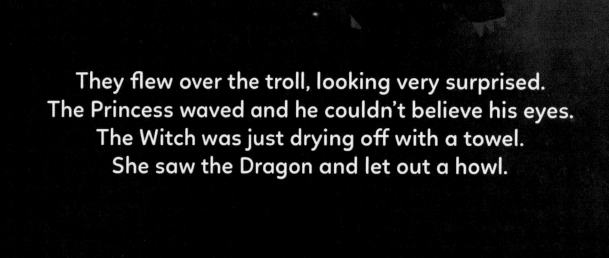

They flew over the troll, looking very surprised.
The Princess waved and he couldn't believe his eyes.
The Witch was just drying off with a towel.
She saw the Dragon and let out a howl.

The Mayor screamed as they swooped over the town.
"A Dragon!" he shouted. "A Dragon, get down!"

They landed by the castle and the guards yelled and fled.
The King shook so much the crown fell off his head.
"Hi mum, hi dad" said the Princess, giving them a wave.
"There really is no reason to be afraid.
This Dragon is friendly and nice and quite sweet.
He really is someone I would like you to meet.
He flew me home so I think it would be rude
if we didn't at least offer him some food."
"Um, ok" said the king in a voice rather small

"Would you like some dinner? It would be no trouble at all."
"Thank you, I would be honoured." replied the Dragon very polite.
They all had a wonderful time that night.

The Princess and the Dragon would meet up and play.
And have different adventures every day.
She thought him scary at first, but he was a Dragon like no other.
Which is why a book should never be judged by its cover.

Printed in Great Britain
by Amazon